GIRLS SURVIVE

Published by Stone Arch Books, an imprint of Capstone.
1710 Roe Crest Drive, North Mankato, Minnesota 56003
capstonepub.com

Library of Congress Cataloging-in-Publication Data is available on the
Library of Congress website
ISBN: 9781669013945 (hardcover)
ISBN: 9781669014454 (paperback)
ISBN: 9781669014461 (ebook PDF)

Summary: After Flor's mother dies in early 1969, she is left with her abuelita who
refuses to accept Flor's identity as a trans girl. Flor decides that in order to be true
to herself, she must leave home. She makes friends with Tami, a trans teenager, and
the two girls meet adults who help them make their way in the queer and trans
community of New York City. Invited to meet up with some new friends, the girls
sneak into the Stonewall Inn on a night that leads to a police raid and violence.
Will Flor escape the riot and continue her fight to live as she is?

Designed by Dina Her

Image Credits
Shutterstock: Heather Shimmin, 108, Okra (geometric pattern) design element
throughout, Spalnic (paper texture) background throughout, timfazyl, 105

Printed and bound in the USA. PO5195

FLOR
FIGHTS BACK

A Stonewall Riots
Survival Story

by Joy Michael Ellison

illustrated by Francesca Ficorilli

STONE ARCH BOOKS
a capstone imprint

CHAPTER ONE

I didn't mean to start a fight with Abuelita. I just missed Mama so badly that I couldn't help myself.

Abuelita made me go to bed early, like she always did now that Mama was gone. I always tried to do what she said, so I turned off my bedroom light and closed my eyes.

I could hear the screech of car brakes and the wail of police sirens from outside my window. The air in my tiny room was hot. It wasn't long before my pillow turned clammy from my sweat.

Sleep didn't come. I had tossed and turned most nights since Mama died six months ago. This was the worst night yet.

After a while, I got up to get a cup of water from the kitchen. I put on my glasses and crept down the hall on my tiptoes, careful not to disturb Abuelita. If she found me out of bed, even just to get a drink, she would yell at me for sure.

The light in my grandma's bedroom was out. Abuelita must be getting the sleep I couldn't. That's when the idea came to me. It wrapped itself around my heart and wouldn't let go.

Instead of sneaking into the kitchen, I opened the door to Mama's room, stepped inside, and then carefully shut it behind me. The room smelled like coffee, cinnamon, and cold cream, like my mom used to.

I turned on the lamp on top of the vanity and then focused my attention to what I had come to see: Mama's big cedar jewelry box. I opened the lid and slowly ran my fingers across the contents inside.

Mama's pearl necklace.

Her gold hoop earrings.

A bracelet of blue beads I made her four years ago, when I was nine.

I traced over the smooth surfaces of the jewelry. I thought of how Mama would let me watch her put on her makeup and pick out her jewelry on Sunday mornings before we went to the cathedral for mass. Sometimes she even let me try on her pearls. She would laugh with delight when I danced around the room for her. She always let me be myself.

My fingers stopped when they reached something soft and silky. It was Mama's purple scarf. She wore it over her curly black hair when it rained. I always thought it made her look elegant, like Rita Moreno or Coretta Scott King.

I picked up the scarf and rubbed it against my cheek. My eyes began to well with tears as I thought about how I would never hug Mama again.

"What are you doing?"

Abuelita was standing in the doorway in her pink robe, her hands on her hips and a scowl etched on her face.

"Nothing," I said. I backed away from the jewelry box, the scarf still in my hand. "I couldn't sleep."

"So, you come in here and disrespect your mother's things?" Abuelita's voice was beginning to rise.

"No," I said. "I just . . ."

"You just want to play with her jewelry like her precious things are your toys. Don't you have any respect for her memory?" Abuelita yelled.

"I d-d-do," I said, stammering. The tears were flowing down my cheeks now.

"I was just remembering how Mama used to let me try on her jewelry," I said.

"Shame on you," said Abuelita. "I've told you a thousand times, you act like a boy while you live in my house. You disgrace your mama and dishonor our family."

Suddenly, my face was hot. Abuelita thought I was a boy because that's what the doctor had said when I was born. That's what everyone saw when they looked at me, but I knew differently. In my heart, I was a girl. I had never told Mama, but she seemed to know anyway. She never cared. Why did Abuelita have to care so much?

I was still crying, but I felt angry too. Angrier than I had ever felt before.

"Mama would want me to have her things!" I yelled. I scrunched her scarf in my hand. "She saw me for who I am."

Abuelita closed her eyes and took a deep breath.

"As long as I am alive, you will conduct yourself as a proper young man," she said. "Now go back to bed. In the morning, I will tell you how much trouble you're in."

I padded back to my room and lay down on my bed.

Grounded. I could handle that. I couldn't stand being someone I wasn't. I wasn't a boy, no matter what my grandma, the doctor, or anyone else said. I was certain that Mama had loved me no matter what.

"I wish you were still here, Mama," I whispered into the darkness. "But since you're not, I know what I have to do."

I waited in the dark until I could hear Abuelita snoring. Slowly, I pushed the covers off me and placed my feet on the floor. Walking to my dresser, I selected a white T-shirt and a pair of bell-bottoms and dressed quickly.

Before putting on my sneakers, I grabbed my backpack and dumped its contents on the bed. I left everything in a heap except for my drawing pencils and my sketchbook. I stuffed those into the backpack.

I listened again to make sure that Abuelita was still asleep. Leaving all the lights out, I stepped out my bedroom door and crept down the hall.

When I passed Mama's room, I stopped for a moment. With all my courage, I dashed into the room and grabbed the purple scarf from her jewelry box.

Back in the hallway, I inched past Abuelita's room and then rushed to the front door of the apartment. I closed it gently and ran down the hallway to the stairs. I kept going until I was out of the apartment building and several blocks away, far from Abuelita.

I was panting like a dog when I stopped running.

I leaned against a greystone building while I caught my breath. After resting for a bit, I looked at the purple scarf in my hand and smiled. I tied it around my neck with two knots to keep it safe. It was my last link to Mama.

I was starting a totally new life. But where would I go?

CHAPTER TWO

I wandered around Greenwich Village for over
an hour, past brownstones, bodegas, and bars. My
mind raced, thinking about the meaning of what
I had done. Yesterday, I was a seventh grader and
the best artist in my art class. Now I was a thirteen-
year-old runaway. I had no money. I couldn't go
home. Where would I sleep?

My feet ached and panic started rising in my
throat. None of the cross streets were familiar.

Mama never let me walk alone this far from our apartment. I was lost.

Suddenly, I heard laughter. I scanned the street to see where it was coming from. A group of teenagers were talking loudly across the way in a small park. Something about them seemed familiar to me, almost comfortable. I felt in my gut that we might have something important in common. I walked toward them.

"You can sit by me."

On a bench near the gaggle of teenagers was a girl who looked a couple years older than me. Her hair was tied up into two neat Afro-puffs. She had a round, cheerful face, but her paisley dress looked dirty. She smiled hesitantly.

"I'm Tami," she said. She held out a hand to me. I shook it.

"Come on, sit down. You look tired," she said.

I obeyed.

"Do you have a name?" asked Tami. "You know, not the name your parents gave you, but one you call yourself? A girl's name?"

"Um," I said, feeling shy. I wondered how she could know that I was a girl. Everyone else looked at my body and saw a boy. No one had ever asked me if I had a name I called myself. I was scared and happy at the same time.

"It's okay," said Tami. "A lot of kids like us hang out here in Sheridan Square and all up and down Greenwich Village. Gay boys," she raised her chin toward two teenagers holding hands. "And girls like me. You know, girls who were born boys?"

Tami suddenly looked worried. She wrapped her arms around her body. "But I don't want to make you uncomfortable."

"I'm not," I said. "But I've never talked about this before. I didn't know there were other people, other girls, you know, like us."

A smile spread over Tami's face as bright as the top of the Empire State Building when it's all lit up at night.

Suddenly words were spilling out of my mouth, words I thought I'd never say.

"I've always wished I had a girl's name. Something pretty, like Flor. That means *flower* in Spanish. I'm Black and Puerto-Rican American," I explained.

People always seemed to want to know where I was from. I didn't fit into the categories that most people are familiar with, but there were lots of mixed kids like me at my school. I waited to see how Tami would react.

"I like it," said Tami. "I'm going to call you Flor, okay?"

"Okay," I said. My heart felt like a bird ready to take flight.

"Don't put your backpack on the ground or even the bench," said Tami. "It's better to hold it so no one can steal it."

I nodded my head and placed my backpack in my lap.

"My dad kicked me out a couple of weeks ago," Tami said. Her brown eyes were sad. "He found me wearing a dress and told me to get out. Did your parents do the same thing?"

"My mom's dead," I said, choking the words out. "My grandma won't let me be me, so I ran away tonight."

I held back tears, but Tami could see the pain I was feeling. She took my hand in hers.

"It's okay," she said. "We can be friends. We can take care of each other."

"Okay," I said.

A smile tugged at my lips. I might have lost my family tonight, but I made friends with someone I had a feeling was going to be very important to me. I wondered if tonight would turn out to be the worst night of my whole life, and one of the best.

I surprised myself by yawning.

Tami laughed. "You've got to be tired. You ready for bed?"

I nodded. "But where do you sleep?"

Tami patted the bench where we were sitting. "It's not so bad," she said. "It's not cold this time of year, and the cops don't usually come to the park."

I gulped.

"Come on," said Tami. "Put your backpack on your back so nothing happens to it. We can lean against each other. It'll be more comfortable that way."

I did as Tami said. It was uncomfortable to lean against my half-empty backpack. Still, I could tell that no one would be able to reach into it. And it was kind of nice putting my head on her shoulder.

"In the morning I'll tell you more about how girls like us get by out here," Tami whispered. "Good night, Flor."

"Good night, Tami."

It still felt good to hear someone say my name out loud as it was the most normal thing in the world. It made me feel real.

I thought I wouldn't be able to sleep after everything that had happened that night. My whole world was completely different, in both good ways and bad.

As I closed my eyes, I wondered about what Tami meant about teaching me how girls like us survive out here. *How were we going to eat? Did Tami have money? Where would we go to the bathroom? Or take a shower? And what did Tami mean about the cops?*

My mind started to spin and whirl, going over everything that there was to worry about. But I could hear Tami's gentle, steady breath, and feel her chest rising and falling. Soon my exhaustion was more powerful than my anxiety. Sleep swept me away.

CHAPTER THREE

Greenwich Village, New York City
Christopher Park
June 27, 1969
6:15 a.m.

My neck ached when my eyes opened in
the morning. Being careful not to wake Tami,
I stretched and tried to work the kinks out of
my sore muscles.

Around me, New York City was already starting
its day. A delivery trunk honked at a man running
across the street. He yelled back and shook his fist
in the air. A group of pigeons cooed and pecked at
the ground for food. One rummaged about in a trash
can until it found a french fry. The other pigeons

mobbed the lucky bird, fighting for a piece of the feast.

For a moment, I thought about joining the fray. My stomach grumbled loudly. I had no idea where or when Tami and I would find something to eat. I would have given anything for the scrambled eggs Mama used to make or the sweet and flaky Pan de Mallorca she bought at Santos Bakery.

I tried to put my hunger out of my mind while I waited for Tami to wake up. She was still snoring softly. To distract myself, I did what I always did when I found myself with time to spare. I opened my backpack and lifted out my sketchbook and a pencil.

My sketchbook wasn't fancy. It was just a pad of plain white paper that Mama brought home from the corner store. I loved it, though. When I drew, I was in complete control. I could create whatever my heart wished. Drawing made me feel safe.

I flipped past my old drawings until I found a blank page. I wondered what to draw. Tami made a small noise and shifted in her sleep. I smiled and began drawing her round cheeks and full lips. Tami's mouth was open ever so slightly, but I drew her with a delicate smile instead.

When I drew portraits, I liked to make people look a tiny bit nicer than they really looked, more like how they pictured themselves or as beautiful as they seemed to me. It was my way of making the world a little sweeter.

I was so absorbed shading my drawing that I didn't notice that Tami had awakened."Is that me?" she asked, leaning over my shoulder.

"Yeah," I said. I shifted my sketchbook away from view, suddenly worried that I had done something wrong. "Is that okay?"

"Okay?" said Tami. "It's better than okay. It's incredible. Do I really look that pretty?"

I blushed. "Yeah, to me at least."

"Is that whole notebook full of your drawings?" asked Tami. "Can I see them?"

I handed Tami the sketchbook and watched as she flipped through the pages. The sketchbook was filled with drawings of models from Mama's magazines, sketches of people I knew, and people I imagined all on my own.

"You're so talented!" squealed Tami. "This gives me an idea. I think I know how we're going to make enough money to buy breakfast. We'll lay out some of your drawings on the sidewalk and sell them!"

"Do you really think people will want to buy them?" I asked.

"I don't know," said Tami. "But we have to try, don't we?"

My stomach rumbled in agreement.

Tami picked out the best drawings she thought

would sell, and I carefully tore them out of my sketchbook. We spread them on the sidewalk at the entry to the park, weighing them down with rocks so that they wouldn't fly away. At Tami's suggestion, I made a sign that said, "Fine art from a real New York City artist, $3 or best offer."

Sitting next to my drawings, I really did feel like a New York City artist, at least for a while.
The feeling didn't last.

Men in business suits, women wearing miniskirts, and teenagers in jeans all walked past without even glancing in our direction. One woman with white hair stopped for a moment, but she scowled when she saw me. Her look made me feel small and helpless. I wanted to give up.

Even Tami was starting to look as depressed as a wilted flower, when we heard a cheerful laugh.

A tall Black woman called out, asking passersby for spare change in a high, nasal voice. She was wearing a blue dress and white sneakers. She had the biggest, brightest smile I had ever seen, and on her head was a crown of flowers. A young man pressed a dollar bill into her hand.

"It's Marsha!" said Tami.

"Who?" I asked.

"Marsha P. Johnson," said Tami, as though I should already know. "The P stands for 'Pay it no mind' because that's how Marsha lives her life. She doesn't pay any mind to what people think about her. Just a second."

Tami waved and rushed over to Marsha. Marsha leaned down and gave the younger girl a hug.

I watched the pair in awe. My mouth dropped open when I saw Marsha hand a wad of crumpled dollar bills and some coins to Tami.

"Do you know that woman?" I asked Tami when she returned. "I mean, is she a friend of yours?"

"Marsha's friends with all of the girls like us," said Tami. "Everybody knows her because she's always sharing whatever she has with other people. She talks about making the world better for us too."

"Really?" I asked.

I could hardly imagine someone giving away money to people they didn't know, even if they had something in common. And I really, *really* couldn't imagine someone believing that they could make things easier for people like me. Boys were boys and girls were girls, at least according to my grandma. People like me didn't even seem to exist. But then, clearly, we did, so who knew that could be possible?

"I told her that you ran away from home just last night and she gave us some money," said Tami. "She says she knows you must be hungry."

I didn't feel good about taking money from someone who also needed it.

We should give it back, I thought. Then my stomach rumbled so loudly that Tami laughed.

"Come on," said Tami. "I'm taking us to breakfast." She gathered up my drawings and handed them to me.

I followed Tami out of the park and down the street. "But if Marsha's always helping out other people, people she doesn't even know, then how does she survive herself?"

"The only way any of us survive is by helping each other," said Tami. "I'll tell you more while we eat. Hurry up!"

Tami took me to a diner a couple of miles north where the waitresses all wore pink dresses and the coffee was free. Tami ordered pancakes, and I had hashbrowns and eggs over easy with lots of hot sauce.

Tami said that most of the kids who lived on the street liked to go to the Howard Johnson's diner because it was big and easy to sneak out without paying. Tami didn't want to steal anything, so we came here where the food was cheaper and everyone was friendly.

"Do we really have enough money?" I asked.

"Don't worry," said Tami. "We're going to be fine. I'm going to tell you everything I've learned about living on the street."

"Are there really a lot of kids like us?" I asked. I could barely imagine there being anyone who felt like me, let alone a whole secret society just a couple of miles from where I grew up.

"Yeah, really," said Tami. "Plenty of kids run away from home or get kicked out by their parents."

My mind reeled. It was like learning that Neverland, Peter Pan, and the Lost Boys were all real. It felt magical, but really sad and scary too.

"Most of the kids out here are gay and, you

know, a little feminine. They're the type of boys who get called 'sissies,' or worse," Tami continued. "And then there are the girls like us. There isn't really a good word for us. Some people call us transvestites—that means someone who has, you know, parts like we do, but wears a dress. I've never liked that word, though. I just think of myself as a girl."

I nodded. "Me too."

Tami poured more syrup on her pancakes. "There are drag queens—that's a man who dresses as a woman some of the time, usually on stage to make money. They hang out in the neighborhood too. We call them "she" when they're in drag, and he when they're out of it. And there are plenty of people who don't fit into any box or fit into more than one. It really doesn't matter. We're all in this together. And it's not like the cops care about the differences between us."

"The cops?" I asked.

"Yeah, the cops," said Tami. "They're always bothering us, for all sorts of reasons. It's illegal for you and me to wear dresses, but you can even get arrested for loitering. That means just being somewhere for longer than the cops like." Tami looked at me, her face serious. "So, if you see a police officer, you run, okay?"

"What happens if you get arrested?" I asked.

"Bad things," said Tami. "They put us in the same cells as men." I could see on her face that it was dangerous. I frowned as I took another bite of my eggs.

"Don't worry, it's not all bad out here," said Tami. "We look out for each other."

Tami explained that almost everyone living on the street shared food and money with each other, just like Marsha had helped us earlier. If one person had a place to stay in a hotel or someone's home, she'd invite her friends. Friends were important here. They became your family.

"It's hard," said Tami. "I'm not going to lie. But it's worth it to be yourself, you know?"

I nodded. I *did* know.

"But someday, somehow, we're going to make things better," said Tami. She looked fierce as she took a huge bite of her pancakes. "I don't know how we'll do it, but I do know that no kid should have to live like we do."

We ate our breakfast slowly, savoring every bite. We sat drinking coffee with tons of sugar until the waitress slammed the check on the table and glared at us.

Tami carefully counted out the money for our bill and left the correct amount on the table. We both went to the bathroom and then stepped out into the sunshine.

As soon as we left the diner, something felt

wrong. There were a few drag queens standing on the corner, looking tense.

When we passed by them, I heard one say, "Here comes Lil."

Tami grabbed my hand. "Run," she said.

CHAPTER FOUR

Tami pulled my arm so hard I made a yelping sound. I was surprised how fast she could run. She led us into an alley, and we sprinted north.

"Stop," I wheezed after a few minutes. "Tami, please."

I wasn't sure if I could run anymore. My breakfast sat heavy in my stomach.

Tami looked around, as though checking to see if anyone was following us. She slowed to a walk.

"Thank you," I said, still panting. "Now, what is going on?"

"Remember how I said that everyone on Christopher Street looks out for each other?" Tami asked. I could tell that she was winded too, even though she hid it better than I did.

I nodded.

Tami continued, "Well, when you hear someone say, 'Here comes Lil,' it means the police are coming."

My eyes grew big.

"Lil is short for the Lilly law." Tami explained. "That's what they call the rules they use to arrest us. We pass the word to each other so that no one gets grabbed. So, if you ever hear anyone saying anything about Lil, you get out of there, you hear?" Tami's expression was serious. Gone was her usual grin.

"It's worse for us," she said. "We're under

eighteen, so that makes us minors. We probably won't be in as much trouble as the older girls. But we're both Black, so, you know, the cops are always looking for people like us."

I did know. Mama had warned me to be careful around the police when I was still in primary school. Because we were Black and Puerto Rican, she explained, the cops were always driving around the neighborhood looking for an excuse to do something. She said that was part of the reason that Abuelita was so strict with me. She always wanted me to come home right after school so that I spent less time out on the street.

But now I had no home to go to. All I had to protect me from the police were my feet and my new friend.

"We've probably run far enough," said Tami. I breathed easier.

We turned right and began making our way out

of the maze of alleys and back to the busy streets of Manhattan, but as we stepped onto 125th Street, I saw the back of another burly police officer.

This time, I grabbed Tami's hand and took off like a shot, running back through the alleys.

We ran for a few minutes when I saw a tall drag queen with a huge blond beehive hairdo. She was casually leaning against the back door of a midsized building. Tami and I nearly ran into her.

"Girls! Watch where you're going!" she snarled, standing up tall.

"Lil," I said. "Here comes Lil."

The drag queen nodded, suddenly serious. "Come inside but be quiet. Hurry up."

We followed the queen through the back door into a hallway full of people, boxes, and racks of sparkly clothing. As we walked, I got a better look at the drag queen's outfit. She wore a short dress and the highest pair of high heels I had ever seen.

She didn't seem all that much older than Tami and me.

"What is this place?" I whispered.

"This is the one and only Apollo Theatre," the drag queen said, waving a hand in a dramatic swooping gesture. "And you're witnessing a rehearsal of the legendary Jewel Box Revue, the best female impersonation show in the country. I'm Jackie," she added.

"I'm Flor," I said, shaking Jackie's hand and glancing around the room. "Female impersonation show?" I asked.

"Well, you're new now, aren't you?" Jackie laughed. "Yes, female impersonation show. All of these lovely ladies you see before you are female impersonators. Drag queens. Including me."

Tami spoke up. "You remember, I told you about them. A female impersonator or a drag queen is a man who gets paid to dress up as a woman and put on a show. They're kind of like us, except that we live as women all the time because that's who we are inside. For them, it's just a costume. Sometimes girls like us work in the shows too."

"And we're all sisters," said Jackie. "At least that's what I think."

I smiled. I never knew there were so many people ready to treat me like family.

"I want you girls to stay here until the police are gone and you've caught your breath," said Jackie. She sounded almost as bossy as Abuelita. "But you have to stay out of the way. We can't have you disrupting rehearsal or letting the producers find you. Now follow me."

I had to hurry to keep up with Jackie. She led us to the wings of the stage and sat us down beside a pile of boxes.

In front of us, half a dozen gorgeous performers in short dresses and huge hats were prancing back and forth across the stage to a jaunty piano tune. They all kicked up their heels at the same time.

"It's amazing, isn't it?" said Jackie. "I wanted to be a movie star when I was little, but then I learned that when you're a gay man like me, there are suddenly no jobs for you. Except for the Jewel Box Revue. It's not what I planned, but I still feel lucky." She sighed.

"I've got to get ready for our number," Jackie added, adjusting her wig. "You stay here, okay?"

Tami and I promised to stay out of the way. While she watched the show, I pulled out my sketchbook and began drawing the performers. Their incredible costumes, covered in feathers and jewels, made them especially fun to draw.

I became so engrossed in my art that I must have lost track of time. I nearly jumped up when I heard Jackie's voice.

"Hey, that's not bad," she said, looking down

at my drawings. "You're pretty good. The queens would love these."

Jackie told me the names of the performers I drew, and I carefully wrote them next to their pictures.

"Who is he? In the black suit?" I asked.

"That's Stormé DeLarverie. He's a she," said Jackie. "She's a male impersonator. That's just like a female impersonator. Instead of being a man dressed as a woman, she's a woman dressed as a man. You get it."

My head was spinning, but I understood. I never knew there were so many ways you could be, so many ways to express how you felt inside. It was amazing.

I knew I wanted to be a girl all the time, but I was happy for boys like Jackie, who enjoyed dressing as women when they wanted. I thought Stormé looked incredible.

"You need to draw me, okay?" Jackie said. She turned to Tami. "Do you know where the Stonewall Inn is?"

Tami nodded. "The bar? It's by Sheridan Square. That's where we slept last night."

Jackie grimaced when she heard where we had been sleeping.

"You come to the Stonewall Inn tonight, and you can draw me and some of the other queens," she said, pointing a slim finger at me. "I bet you could make a few bucks on these drawings. And then you can come home with me and sleep on my floor. I can't have you young ladies sleeping on a park bench."

Jackie led us through the hubbub of backstage and back to the door to the alley, telling us goodbye before heading back inside.

I was feeling better than I had in a while. There was just one thing bothering me.

"Tami?" I asked. "You said that the Stonewall Inn is a bar, right?"

"Uh-huh," agreed Tami.

"But we're too young for a bar. How will we get in?"

CHAPTER FIVE

Tami answered my question with a laugh. She explained that it was easy to sneak into the Stonewall Inn. In the city of New York, it was illegal to serve alcohol to gay and lesbian people.

Of course, people like us—people who wore clothes that matched their sense of self, but not with other people's expectations—weren't welcome anywhere. So, the bars that did let us in were acting outside the law. The mafia ran most of them, and they didn't bother to check IDs.

"When you're already breaking a dozen laws, what's another few?" Tami laughed.

She seemed so confident. She reminded me of a picture of Nefertiti that I saw in a book about Ancient Egypt I checked out of the library when I was in third grade. I wished I were that sure of myself, but going to a bar run by mobsters made me nervous.

Still, I wanted to see Jackie again and take him up on his offer to let us stay with him. The thought of spending another night on a park bench turned my stomach.

So, after a long, slow walk through Central Park and another unsuccessful attempt to sell my drawings, Tami led us south down 6th Avenue toward Christopher Street.

The sky was dark, but the city air was still muggy and hot. I was feeling tired, and I wished we had taken a nap in the green grass of Central

Park. But when we arrived at our destination, my exhaustion disappeared.

The Stonewall Inn was a brick building with a huge marquee sign hanging in front for all to see. The lights reading "Stonewall" shone bright, like a lighthouse guiding all people like me safely to a shore where we could be ourselves. Standing in front of the heavy wooden door, my knee wobbled in fear, but my stomach fluttered in eager anticipation.

"You ready?" Tami grinned. I nodded and we stepped through the bar's arched doorway and into a new world.

A bored-looking man sitting by the door eyed us up and down. Tami was right; he didn't ask for our IDs. He just motioned to a book where we were supposed to sign our names. I wrote mine, but Tami wrote down "Minnie Mouse." I felt like Dorothy walking into Oz when we finally entered the bar.

I was surprised how crowded the Stonewall Inn was. People were packed together, whether on barstools, clustered around the jukebox, or on the dance floor. I had no idea there could be so many people like me in a bar facing onto a major street in Greenwich Village.

The second thing I noticed about the Stonewall Inn was that it was loud. In the corner, a group of glamorous women in short skirts laughed, letting out high-pitched squeals of delight. By the bar, skinny white boys yelled drink orders to the bartenders. I thought I heard a glass break.

Over it all, the jukebox blasted a drumroll. Then the harmonies of a familiar set of voices burst out, like an angel choir. It was Sly and the Family Stone, my mama's favorite band. I stood a little taller and a smile spread across my face.

Somehow Jackie's voice cut through the commotion.

"Flor, Tami," she called. "Come on! Get over here, girlies."

Jackie was wearing a sliver minidress and white go-go boots. Instead of a blond bouffant, her hair was now brown with thick bangs, and it fell all the way to her waist.

I wondered if it was a wig, but my mama taught me to never ask that question to any woman, and I figured it was the same for drag queens. Hair was personal and if it looked good, it hardly mattered where it came from.

Jackie was fingering the rim of a tall, slender glass with a clear liquid. The glass looked a little dingy to me, but Jackie didn't seem to mind.

"We've heard about your little drawings, honey," a queen with a deep voice sitting next to Jackie said to me. "I would love to see them. Jackie tells me you're very talented."

"Thank you," I said, suddenly feeling shy.

"You sit over here by me," said Jackie. "Scoot over, Lynn."

Tami and I sat down, squeezing in close to Jackie. I strained to open my backpack and spread out my paper and pencils.

The music changed. It was "Build Me Up, Buttercup," by the Foundations.

Tami squealed, her eyes wide with delight. "I love this song!"

"You want to dance, darling?" asked Jackie.

Tami nodded.

"Well, don't be shy," said Jackie. "You get out there. I'll follow you."

"I'll watch your things," said the drag queen named Lynn. I shook my head and put my backpack on. It was a little awkward, but I didn't want to let it out of my sight.

Tami headed straight toward the dance floor, pulling me behind her. Jackie followed behind us.

Tami and I held hands, bouncing up and down in time to the music. I felt free, like the little girl that I had always wanted to be.

Then the jukebox stopped playing and all lights in the bar went on, bright and strong.

"Police," I heard a voice say. "We're taking the place."

CHAPTER SIX

Greenwich Village, New York City
The Stonewall Inn
June 28, 1969
1:20 a.m.

"Stay close to me," Jackie said into my ear.

My eyes blinked away the shock to my system.
I could feel a new current of tension spread
throughout the bar.

All the couples that had been standing close to
each other were far apart now. Smiles were replaced
with wrinkled brows and stiff lips. Many people had
turned to someone of the opposite gender, acting
like they had been dancing together all along. I
wondered if it was illegal to dance with someone of
the same gender. I guessed yes.

I caught the gaze of a woman in tight jeans and a black T-shirt. Her brown eyes were worried. I thought of what Tami had told me about what happened to girls like us in prison. I wondered if it was as bad for the lesbians who wore masculine clothes. Judging by the expression on this woman's face, it must be.

Jackie put a hand on my shoulder. "We have to get out of here. Now."

I could tell by the tone in her voice that this was serious. She started steering me toward the back of the bar.

I followed Jackie, but I kept looking back over my shoulder to see what the cops were doing. A couple of policemen were ordering people into lines. The cops traced the bodies of the patrons with their eyes.

The way they looked at the drag queens and women like us made me squirm. They checked IDs and ordered some of the patrons to one side. I heard the clink of handcuffs.

The patrons looked like they were scared and angry, but they were clearly used to this procedure. They cooperated until a police officer approached a Black woman. She was tall and wearing white tennis shoes. I thought she might have been Marsha P. Johnson.

"ID," barked a police officer, not making eye contact.

The woman shook her head slowly. The officer glanced up, confusion on his face.

"I got my civil rights," said the woman, her voice ringing out like a bell. She reached back like a baseball pitcher and threw a shot glass at a mirror behind the bar. The mirror shattered with a spectacular crashing noise.

When the mirror broke, it was as though a spell had been broken. The patrons of the Stonewall no longer looked meek. Some people began yelling at the police. I heard someone shout "gay power."

"Flor!" snapped Jackie. "Come on." Jackie pushed me in front of her and propelled us toward the exit at the back of the bar. I turned my head to look over my shoulder one more time, but all I could see was the fear in Jackie's face.

We stepped out in the alley. The world outside of the bar felt strange. There was a feeling in the air, an electric energy that made me believe something was about to happen.

Jackie turned toward the front of the Stonewall Inn and began walking back to Christopher Street. Before the street came into view, I could hear the noise of a crowd and see the blue flashing of police-car lights. The night air was hot, but I shivered.

In front of the Stonewall Inn, the police were dragging a light-skinned Black woman in a suit toward a police wagon.

"Don't be so rough," she said to the police officer.

The officer responded by hitting her in the head with his billy club. He looked surprised when the woman began fighting back with all her strength. She yelled and cursed and punched and kicked. The police officer struggled to keep ahold of her.

"Oh my lord," said Jackie. "That's Stormé!"

I looked again and realized that Jackie was right. It was Stormé DeLarverie, the drag king from the Jewel Box Review.

The police grabbed Stormé again, but once again she pushed them off. The crowd stared, stunned. She turned and her piercing gaze surveyed the crowd.

"Why don't you do something?" she yelled.

For the second time that evening, the energy changed. The crowd responded with a roar.

Someone began throwing glass beer bottles. A wave of anger surged around me.

That's when I realized that Tami wasn't by my side. I looked around desperately, but she was nowhere to be seen.

CHAPTER **SEVEN**

"Tami!" I screamed, but my voice barely pierced the growing noise.

The crowd was growing steadily, filling Christopher Street. Where were all these people coming from? News of what was happening in front of the Stonewall Inn must have spread to everyone living in Greenwich Village, but how did the word travel so fast?

"Tami!" I called again, looking around wildly.

Beside me a boy in jean shorts was yelling at the police, saying words that would get me in serious trouble if my abuelita heard me saying them. A queen in a low-cut dress was bending down to pick up a brick. She heaved it toward a police car. The windshield shattered, sending glass flying. A police officer lunged at her. He grabbed her wrist and began kicking her in the stomach.

My heart was pounding. How could I have lost Tami? Where could she be now?

"Copper for a copper!" I heard someone behind me shout.

A penny flew through the air and hit a policeman's helmet. Laughter erupted all around me. Suddenly a burst of loose change hailed down on the cops standing by the police wagon. They tried to duck.

I raised my hands to cover my face to protect myself from the pennies, bricks, and glass bottles flying around me. I pushed past someone who was trying to lift a garbage can to throw it at a cop car. Someone else stepped on my toes and I yelped in pain.

As the crowd grew, it surged forward and back like a wave. I felt like I was fighting against the current, but I had to get to the edge of the crowd. I had to look for Tami. I would not leave her behind. I would not lose her.

I finally reached the sidewalk in front of the Stonewall Inn and paused to catch my breath. I scanned the crowd, searching for a glimpse of Tami's twists or her round face. I stood on my tiptoes, straining to see over the sea of faces. The crowd looked angry, elated, and afraid all at the same time.

I was too worried about Tami to take it in, though. If she wasn't in the crowd, could she still be in the Stonewall Inn?

I started my way toward the alley leading to the back door that Jackie and I had used to escape. If Tami was still in there, then I was going to get her out. She would never leave me on my own. I wasn't about to abandon her.

"Child, what do you think you're doing?" The voice stopped me in my tracks.

Jackie stepped in front of me, hands on her hips. She blocked the entrance to the alley.

"Tami must still be in there," I said, trying to push past Jackie. "We have to save her."

Jackie's face was grim. "If she's still inside, there's nothing we can do."

Jackie pointed toward the Stonewall Inn. "Look."

Flames were licking the side of the building. I watched as a bottle stuffed with a burning piece of cloth flew through the air. It landed among the open flames with a crash.

The bottle must have been filled with alcohol or gasoline because the flames grew higher and higher.

"Tami," I screamed again.

I thrashed against Jackie, desperately trying to push my way past her.

"Hush," she whispered in my ear. "If Tami is still in there, the police have her. We can't do anything except stay safe ourselves."

"The police have barricaded themselves inside the bar," someone yelled.

I saw a group of protestors lifting a parking meter and beating it against the front door of the bar. The crash of metal on wood was terrible to hear.

A crowd of police—the cops that had originally entered the inn—were emerging from the smoke-filled bar. They dragged a group of handcuffed people behind them. Standing near the back of the line was a short, dark-skinned girl with a face the shape of the moon and two Afro-puffs on her head. She was coughing. A police officer gripped her arm.

"Tami," I screamed again.

Jackie was right. She was under arrest.

CHAPTER EIGHT

Without thinking, I lunged toward Tami, reaching my hand out for her. It wasn't a wise thing to do, I realized later. How did I think I could possibly help her without getting arrested myself?

But something amazing happened. The crowd around me surged toward Tami and the other arrestees. They kicked and punched and pulled the police off them.

I grabbed Tami and hugged her tight.

"Are you okay?" I asked as I dragged her away from the police and toward the center of the crowd.

"I'm fine," Tami said with a laugh. "Thanks to you."

"Well," I said, "girls like us stick together." We hugged again.

Tami threaded her arm through mine and turned to look around at the scene surrounding us. "Wow," she exclaimed. "This is incredible."

Sirens cut through the noise of the crowd. I watched as more police cars and wagons pulled up. When the police reinforcements stepped from their vehicles, I saw that some of them were wearing heavy helmets. One flipped down his plastic visor. His jaw was set as hard as a rock, and his eyes were steely.

To our left a pair of teenagers was teasing a police officer, making oinking noises and extending their middle fingers. Gone from their faces was the hesitant, apologetic look I had seen on the faces of so many kids living on Christopher Street. I had felt it on my own face, the fear and shame that made me want to hang my head and slink away so that no one could see me.

It was a terrible, heavy feeling, that sense of something being wrong with me. But that burden had melted away. It was replaced by a righteous anger at the police who chased and arrested and beat us for no reason.

I heard a whooping noise to my right and looked over my shoulder. Standing next to me was Marsha P. Johnson in her white sneakers and dazzling smile. Her dress was torn, but her crown of pink and white roses and silver beads was still perched perfectly atop her head.

She was standing with an arm wrapped through the elbow of another woman, just like Tami and me. The other woman was shorter than Marsha and had a sharp, elegant nose. Her mane of curly brown hair and fierce expression reminded me of a lioness.

"The revolution!" she shouted in a Puerto-Rican American accent. "It's beautiful."

I realized that the woman with the accent I knew so well was right. The streets weren't just filled with anger. We were alive with hope. We were fighting back for a better future, where kids like me would never have to sleep on park benches. Where they would never be made to choose between their families and being true to themselves. We were defending ourselves against the police who stole our dreams and trampled our rights.

"Viva la revolución!" I shouted. "Long live the revolution!"

The crowd around me answered my cry with whoops and hollers. A few voices shouted "Revolution!" I laughed with delight. I had never imagined myself leading a crowd in protest.

I felt powerful, a part of something, and able to make a difference.

I felt a gentle hand on my shoulder. I looked up to see Jackie, grinning down at me. She had her arm linked with another drag queen. A woman grabbed Tami's arm and suddenly we were a part of a line of dancing people, kicking in unison, just like the Rockettes at Radio City Music Hall.

We danced our way toward the line of police who, to my surprise, looked terrified of us. Burly officers holding wooden clubs stepped back as we approached, their eyes wide with shock. For a few moments, the police seemed frozen in place, until one started charging toward us and the others followed. They grabbed at us, and my heart nearly stopped.

As quickly as the kick line had assembled, it broke up. Jackie kept holding my hand, though.

"Don't worry," she said. "Just follow me."

Jackie began running, and I sprinted after her, pulling Tami after me. Jackie led us down the street away from the police. When we reached the corner of Christopher Street and Waverly Place, we took a sharp right and then another one, running in a triangular path. With another turn, we were back on Christopher Street on the opposite side of the police line. The cops looked around in confusion.

Someone began to chant, and the queens around me took up the call:

> *"We are the Stonewall girls*
> *We wear our hair in curls*
> *We wear our dungarees*
> *Above our nelly knees!"*

I laughed and whooped and kicked up my heels. I couldn't have felt better if I were onstage at the Apollo Theater with the Jewel Box Revue.

CHAPTER **NINE**

The humid air of Christopher Street was still electric with excitement and possibility, but the crowd in front of the Stonewall Inn was starting to shrink. I found myself yawning.

"Okay, girlies," said Jackie. "Time to take you home like I promised."

Tami and I started to protest, but our voices sounded meek and halfhearted. We had grown too tired to put up much of a fight.

"None of that," said Jackie. She put an arm around each of us and started leading us away. "I'm betting that the cops are going to start clearing us out, since they aren't as outnumbered as before. We're all lucky not to be in a holding cell. Don't you want to keep it that way?"

I nodded. My feet hurt. Sleeping on the floor inside a safe apartment sounded as luxurious as the Waldorf Astoria hotel. I hoped that Jackie had some food too.

We followed Jackie north up 7th Avenue, toward the Empire State Building. Jackie said that the walk wasn't long, but with every step, I realized more clearly just how tired and hungry I was. When we turned onto 23rd Street, Jackie led us to a dingy building called the Chelsea Hotel. I heaved a sigh of relief.

The man sitting behind the front desk didn't seem to be surprised to see Jackie returning home after four in the morning. He just gave us a single nod, and we began climbing the stairs.

Jackie's third-floor apartment was nearly empty, but it would have been clean enough to please Abuelita. We made peanut butter and jelly sandwiches. I ate mine quickly and then wished I had savored it.

Jackie took the blanket and pillows off his bed and arranged them on the floor, making a comfortable spot for Tami and me.

"Good night, girls," he said. "I wish you sweet dreams."

I lay down next to Tami and soon I could hear her soft breath rising and falling in a relaxed, even rhythm. I closed my eyes, but the dreams Jackie wished for me didn't come. Instead, I thought about my future.

Would the riot outside of the Stonewall Inn change things for Tami and me? Would one night of protest be enough to make the police leave us alone? I doubted it.

Images from the riot flooded my mind. Stormé pushing the police officer off her. The police car with the smashed windshield. Angry, defiant faces in the crowd. The cries of "gay power." It had been a scary, confusing evening, but beautiful too. I wished other people could see it like I did, especially the other street kids who weren't there.

Then I realized that maybe they could.

Careful not to wake Tami, I wriggled out from underneath the blanket. I reached for my backpack, which was lying next to our makeshift bed.

Trying not to make a sound, I crept to the kitchen table. I opened up my backpack, wincing at the sound of the zipper. I looked into the other room. Tami and Jackie continued sleeping peacefully. I flipped open my sketchbook, gripped my pencil, and began to draw.

Soon the page was alive and filled with a picture of Tami escaping from the back of the police wagon, Marsha and her friend with their fists raised in the air, and Jackie and me dancing in a glorious kick line.

In bubble letters across the top of the page, I wrote, "June 28, 1969: The night we fought for our rights." I smiled to myself and across the bottom I wrote, "Viva la revolución!"

Not bad, I thought.

8:45 a.m.

I woke up to a smell I knew well: scrambled eggs.

"Get up, sleepy. And come on in here," called Jackie from the kitchen. "You've got some explaining to do."

I pushed the blanket off me and got up from the floor, stretching a bit. Mama and Abuelita raised me right, so I picked up the blanket and spread it across Jackie's bed and replaced the pillows Tami and I had used.

"Come on," said Jackie. "Don't you want breakfast?"

I hurried to the kitchen where Tami was already sitting at the table with a plate of toast in front of her.

"There she is, our little Miss Andy Warhol." Jackie placed a cast-iron skillet of eggs on the center of the table.

"Huh?" I asked.

"We saw your drawing," said Tami. "It's really, really good."

"Oh," I said, suddenly embarrassed. "I just wanted to show people who weren't there last night what really happened. I thought it might be good for other kids like us to know."

Jackie and Tami both nodded their heads.

"That's a really good idea," said Tami.

"Yeah, but it's not like one drawing can really do that," I said, shrugging.

"I don't know," said Jackie as he loaded eggs on a plate and placed it in front of me. "You've given me an idea. Now eat your breakfast, both of you. I'm going to go make a phone call."

Jackie put on his go-go boots and dug in his wallet for change. He explained that he was going to the pay phone outside the hotel and would be back in a couple of minutes.

While we waited for him to return, Tami and I stuffed our faces with toast and eggs. Jackie's eggs were almost as good as Mama's, but I wished he had hot sauce.

When Jackie burst back into his apartment, he had a sly smile on his face.

"Flor," he said. "Do you trust me?"

I nodded. "You gave us a place to sleep and fed us. Of course I trust you."

"Enough to let me borrow this?" he asked, picking up my drawing.

I hesitated but nodded again.

"Good," said Jackie. "I'll be back in half an hour."

CHAPTER **TEN**

Chelsea, New York City
Jackie's apartment
June 28, 1969
9:15 a.m.

When Jackie returned, he flung open the door and shouted, "Guess what?"

"What?" asked Tami.

Jackie twirled his way to us, as though his apartment was the Apollo Theater stage. He was holding a stack of papers in his hands, which fluttered as he danced.

"You wanted other people to know what happened last night, right?" said Jackie. "Well,

I called a friend of mine who always knows everybody's business. He says that people are planning on protesting in front of the Stonewall Inn again tonight. And then I called another friend who works at a printshop, and he hooked us up with . . . ," Jackie paused for dramatic effect, "these!"

Jackie handed the stack of papers to me. It was my drawing, photocopied dozens of times.

"Jackie, how did you pay for this?" I asked.

Jackie waved a hand in front of his face, as though brushing away my question. "Don't worry about it," he said. "Let's just say my friend got a good deal."

"We can flyer Christopher Street!" said Tami. "I bet a lot of the other kids will come to the protest tonight if we tell them about it."

"Uh-huh," said Jackie, his eyes twinkling. "That's exactly what I was thinking."

A smile spread across my face. I felt as excited

as I had the night before when we danced in front of the police.

Greenwich Village, New York City
10:00 a.m.

Jackie had to go to the Apollo Theater for rehearsal, so he left the apartment after taking a shower and telling us to meet him at the park by the Stonewall Inn at sunset. Tami and I cleaned up and then we hit the streets with our flyers.

Tami led the way, half walking, half skipping down the street. I almost had to run to keep up with her.

"I'm going to take us to all the spots along Christopher Street where people like us hang out!" she squealed. "Starting with the piers!"

We made it to the Christopher Street Piers in record time, and Tami immediately walked straight up to a group of teenagers and pressed a flyer into a boy's hand. I was shy and hesitant to talk to people I didn't know, but Tami was fearless. She told everyone we met to meet at the Stonewall Inn that evening.

Some of the people we talked to didn't seem all that interested, but most perked up when they saw my drawing. A few recognized Tami from the picture and asked her about her escape from the police. One girl even asked if she could have a few more flyers for her friends.

By the end of the day, my feet ached. We were tired, but I couldn't wait to get to the Stonewall Inn to see what would happen that night.

"Flor, I think tonight's going to be huge," said Tami.

"I think you might be right, Tami," I said.

We passed out our last flyer to a girl that was even younger than me. She looked at the picture with awe in her eyes.

"Will you come tonight?" asked Tami.

The girl bit her lip. "Maybe," she said. She carefully folded the flyer into fourths and placed it in her pocket. It seemed as important to her as my mama's scarf was to me.

With the last of the flyers gone, we began making our way to the park near the Stonewall Inn.

"Let's pass by the bar," said Tami. "I really want to see what it looks like today."

I was ready to sit down in the park and take a nice long break, but Tami looked excited. I had to admit, I was curious too.

The front window of the Stonewall Inn was boarded up. Large white letters were neatly painted on the plywood.

"We homosexuals plead with our people to

WE HOMOSEXUALS PLEAD WITH
OURPEOPLE TO PLEASE HELP
MAINTAIN PEACEFUL AND QUIET
CONDUCT ON THE STREETS
THE VILLAGE - MATTACHINE

please help maintain peaceful and quiet conduct on the streets of the village," Tami read out loud. "It's signed Mattachine. You don't know what that means, do you?"

"The Mattachine Society is a secret organization for men who love other men," said a familiar voice behind us.

"Jackie!" I said.

"Hiya," he answered. "I guess Mattachine isn't so secret anymore. Nothing about our lives is ever going to be hidden again. I'm all for peace, but if they think I'm going to be quiet, they're in for a shock."

"From now on, we fight back," I said.

"Yeah, yeah," said Tami. "Of course, we will, but for now can we please just sit down for a while?"

I laughed and we turned to walk toward Sheridan Square where Tami and I met. The three of us sat down on the bench where we slept on my first night on the street.

As the sun began to set, the park started to fill up with street kids, queens, lesbians, and gay men. I recognized a few of them from earlier in the day. There were even a few Black men and women in leather jackets and berets. Jackie said they were members of a radical organization called the Black Panthers. I thought they looked tough and beautiful, exactly the way I wanted to be.

I watched as the crowd around us grew. A few people held our flyers.

I ran my fingers across the purple scarf around my neck. It was amazing how much my life had changed in just two days. I lost my home, but I gained a family who loved me.

"You know," said Tami, "We helped bring all these people together. We did this, Flor."

"Yeah," I said.

An unfamiliar feeling welled up inside me. It was a feeling of being powerful.

"If we can do this," I said, "what else might be possible?"

A NOTE FROM THE AUTHOR

The Stonewall Riots were an important turning point in the struggle for lesbian, gay, bisexual, and transgender, queer, intersex, and Two-Spirit (LGBTQIA2) rights. The protests represented an explosion of anger from a community that was tired of unfair treatment, humiliation, arrest, and violence. (For definitions for the terms that make up the acronym LGBTQIA2, visit my website, jmellison.net/books/gender-resources-for-parents-and-teachers/lgbtqia2/)

The riots were not, however, the beginning of the movement. The everyday struggle to survive waged by young queer and transgender people, like Flor and Tami, was just as an important a part of LGBTQIA2 history.

Flor and Tami are fictional characters, but their problems were—and remain—very real for many young transgender girls of color. In 1969, many LGBTQIA2 young people were kicked out of their homes, like Tami. Others were forced to flee them, like Flor. Many heard

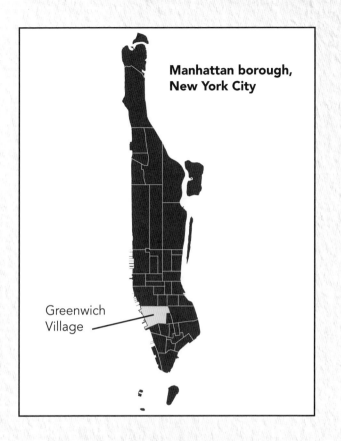

Manhattan borough, New York City

Greenwich Village

stories and rumors about communities of youth like them and found their way to neighborhoods like Greenwich Village.

Once transgender girls of color arrived on Christopher Street, they faced all of the problems that unhoused young people continue to face today. They also had to confront racism, homophobia, and transphobia.

As Tami explained, it was illegal for transgender girls to wear feminine clothing. Police officers who wanted to arrest them could easily find excuses to do so. Transgender girls were charged with loitering, vagrancy, and many other crimes.

To survive, LGBTQIA2 youth supported each other. Like Tami and Flor, they shared food, information, and other resources. When I read interviews with them, it became clear that they were brave, creative, funny, and strong. When I began writing this book, I wanted to make sure that Flor and Tami reflected the vibrant intelligence and determination of the real girls who inspired their story.

While Tami, Flor, and Jackie are works of fiction, other characters in this book are very real. Marsha P. Johnson was an important member of the Christopher Street community. She was legendary for her acts of kindness, like the ones she showed Tami and Flor. Stormé DeLarverie was a biracial lesbian and the host of the Jewel Box Revue. Marsha's unnamed friend with the Puerto Rican accent is Sylvia Rivera, an important transgender liberation activist.

Both Stormé and Marsha were present at the Stonewall Riots. Stormé is widely acknowledged to have been the first person to fight back against the police. Although many people witnessed her bravery, she never confirmed the story. She thought it was more important to emphasize that the entire community participated in the protests that night.

For many years, Marsha was credited with throwing a shot glass at a police officer, but she denied it. I include the incident because I love the story and the ways that the Stonewall Riots have become larger than life.

It's impossible to know exactly what happened the first night of the Stonewall Riots. Anyone who has been a part of a large protest or present at a disaster knows that they can be confusing and complicated. Many different stories have been told about the Stonewall Riots, making it perfect for historical fiction.

Historians, however, do agree that transgender women of color, including young girls like Flor and Tami, played pivotal roles during the protests. Gay white men, especially young drag queens like Jackie, were also present during the riots. They were joined by lesbians,

Today the Stonewall Inn is recognized as a National Historic Landmark.

like Stormé, and people from all parts of the LGBTQIA2 community.

Learning about the Stonewall Riots and the LGBTQIA2 liberation movement makes me proud to be a nonbinary transgender person. We owe Stormé, Marsha, Sylvia, and the unnamed transgender girls who lived lives like Tami and Flor's our respect and deep gratitude.

MAKING CONNECTIONS

1. Tami says to Flor, "We look out for each other." What problems do Flor and Tami face as transgender girls of color who live on the streets? How do the characters in this book work together to help each other survive and solve their problems?

2. The Stonewall Riots involved LGBTQIA2 people of many different identities and experiences. Write down a list of characters in this story. What do they have in common? How are they different? What allows them to develop relationships with each other? Explain your answers.

3. Flor uses her talents as an artist to share information about what happened during the Stonewall Riots and invite other LGBTQIA2 youth to come to a protest. Think of a social cause that is important to you. What talents can you use to share information about it? Write down a plan for using your talent to invite people to take action in support of your cause.

GLOSSARY

Andy Warhol (AN-dee WAR-haul)—Andy Warhol was a gay artist famous for his paintings, films, and magazines. He was born in Pittsburgh, Pennsylvania, August 6, 1928. He spent his adult life in New York City until he died February 22, 1987.

drag king (DRAYG KING)—a person who dresses up in masculine clothes as a part of a performance. A drag king is usually a woman. Nonbinary people can also be drag kings. Today, some men perform as drag kings as well, but that was not common during Flor's time. Some drag kings wear masculine clothes offstage, but they identify as women. Stormé was one such drag king. She often wore men's suits, but she understood herself to be a lesbian woman.

drag queen (DRAYG KWEEN)—a person who dresses up in feminine clothes as a part of a performance. A drag queen is usually a man. Nonbinary people can also be drag queens. Today, some women perform as drag queens as well, but that was not common during Flor's time. Some drag queens wear feminine clothes offstage, but they identify as men. Jackie was one such drag queen.

female impersonator (FEE-mayl im-PUR-suh-nay-ter)—see drag queen. The term *female impersonator* was used during Flor's lifetime, but it is no longer used.

gay (GAY)—describing a person who is attracted to people of their gender. A man, woman, or nonbinary person can be gay.

lesbian (LEZ-bee-uhn)—a woman who is attracted to other women. Nonbinary people can also identify with this term.

loitering (LOI-ter-ing)—spending a long time in a public place. Loitering is a crime. Because it does not have a very specific definition, police officers can use it to arrest people they would prefer were not present in public spaces. Transgender women and girls of color, like Flor and Tami, were often arrested for loitering during the 1960s. Unhoused LGBTQIA2 young people are still regularly arrested for loitering today.

male impersonator (MAYL im-PUR-suh-nay-ter)—see drag king. The term male impersonator was used during Flor's lifetime but is no longer used.

transgender (trans-JEN-der)—a person whose gender identity is different from their gender identity assigned at birth. Nonbinary people are also transgender. They can be born with any type of body.

vagrancy (VAY-gruhn-see)—being unhoused or homeless. Vagrancy is a crime. Transgender women and girls of color, like Flor and Tami, were often arrested for vagrancy during the 1960s. Many vagrancy laws have been overturned, but unhoused people are still harassed and arrested by police today.

ABOUT THE AUTHOR

Joy Michael Ellison is a doctor of women's, gender, and sexuality studies and an assistant professor at Rhode Island University. They are the author of *Sylvia and Marsha Start a Revolution*, a picture book about Sylvia Rivera, Marsha P. Johnson, and the Stonewall Riots. Joy loves watching birds, listening to vinyl records, and being a part of movements for social justice.

ABOUT THE ILLUSTRATOR

Francesca Ficorilli was born and lives in Rome, Italy. Francesca knew she wanted to be an artist since she was a child. She was encouraged by her love for animation and her mother's passion for fine arts. After earning a degree in animation, she started working as a freelance animator and illustrator. She finds inspirations for her illustrations in every corner of the world.